A huge thank you to Janetta and Judith
for their continued faith in me, to my family for their support
and to Swayam, Natu and his family for welcoming me.

This book describes a real wedding, photographed by Prodeepta Das
in Janla and Puri, in the eastern Indian state of Odisha.
While many of the customs are common to all Hindu weddings in India
and abroad, there are some local variations, such as the sprinkling
of holy water from the village temple. The influence of Bollywood
is evident in music sound systems and dance; in past times the
predominant music would have been provided by
traditional Indian instruments and drums.

JANETTA OTTER-BARRY BOOKS

Text and photographs copyright © Prodeepta Das 2014

The right of Prodeepta Das to be identified as the author and photographer
of this work has been asserted by him in accordance with the
Copyright, Designs and Patents Act, 1988 (United Kingdom).

First published in Great Britain and in the USA in 2014 by
Frances Lincoln Children's Books,
74-77 White Lion Street, London N1 9PF
www.franceslincoln.com

A catalogue record for this book is available from the British Library.

ISBN 978-1-84780-446-4

Set in Apollo MT

Printed in China

1 3 5 7 9 8 6 4 2

A Day I Remember

Remember

An Indian Wedding

Prodeepta Das

F

FRANCES LINCOLN
CHILDREN'S BOOKS

My name is Swayam, and I'm going to tell you about the amazing day I went to my uncle Natu Mamu's wedding.

First we went to Janla, my mum's village, where my *aai* (grandmother) and mum told me some exciting news: I had been chosen, out of all the children, to be Natu Mamu's *markundi*. The *markundi* gets to wear special clothes and goes with the groom to the bride's house. He is the most important person after the bride and the groom. I was very happy!

The day before the wedding is called *Mangan*. Our family's house was washed and decorated. Duni Aai (Grandma Duni), the oldest married woman in our family, was in charge of all the wedding preparations.

The women gathered in the courtyard to have *alata* (a red vegetable dye) put on their feet.

The girls had *mehndi* (henna) patterns put on their hands — and I had one too!

To celebrate the wedding, Duni Aai had drawn holy Hindu
designs in the centre of the courtyard. My friend, Chintu,
and I wanted to get close, but Duni Aai shooed us away.

"Don't step on the designs, or you will never be able to marry,"
she warned us. So we stepped back and watched from the side.

Next morning was the wedding day.

I heard drums beating and the sound of a conch.

The *baradhara* (the bride's brother), was coming to

invite the bridegroom, Natu Mamu, to the wedding.

Natu Mamu sat on a small stool while Duni Aai tapped
his knee, shoulders and head with a stone pestle.
"This will make him strong to look after his wife and
family," she said. Then she sprinkled holy water from
the temple over Natu Mamu.

Natu Mamu and I both had *chandon* (sandalwood paste) put on our foreheads in a special wedding pattern, and then *alata* were put on our feet.

We changed into our very special clothes and had our picture taken with Natu Mamu's mum and dad. I really liked the turban. It made me look like a prince.

In the afternoon, we set out for Puri, where the wedding was going to take place. Chintu and the rest of our family went by coach. As *markundi*, I sat with Natu Mamu in the wedding car. It made me feel important, but I missed Chintu.

As we drove along, musicians played drums and *shehnai*, sacred instruments which are always played at Indian weddings.

It was evening when we reached Puri. The musicians played songs from Hindi films and some of the guests danced all the way to the wedding.

The bride's father and their priest welcomed Natu Mamu, touching his head with a coconut for a happy life.

Then all the guests were served dinner – fried rice, chappati, dal, meat curry, salad and crispy popadoms. It was delicious!

At last we were ready to begin the wedding.

Natu Mamu and his bride, Salina, sat opposite
each other, while the priest tied their hands
together and chanted sacred hymns. They were
given colourful headdresses called *mukuta*.

Then the bride and the groom walked
round the holy fire seven times.

Natu Mamu and Salina repeated after the priest
their promises to love and look after each other.
Now they were married!

It was almost morning when we arrived back at our village.
All the women welcomed Natu Mamu and his new wife by
lighting a holy lamp, and they played a traditional game of
cowrie shells. In the old days, cowrie shells were used as
coins. So the game is about being careful with money.

I sat with my new *maain* (auntie) as guests came
to see her and give presents. She wore a beautiful saree,
lots of gold jewellery and special red bangles called
shankhaa, to show that she was now a married woman.

This was followed by a big feast of meat curry,
fried fish, fried vegetables, chappati and yoghurt salad.
All the food was freshly cooked in front of us.
There was a long queue for the desserts. Ice cream and
hot *jelabis* (yellow syrupy sweets) were my favourites!

At last the wedding was over. It was the
most exciting day I can ever remember.
I can't wait to be a *markundi* again!